L is for Leprechaun

an ABC book
of Notre Dame.

written by Barbara Gowan and illustrated by Jane Pitz

Learning With Little Folks
PO Box 5674
Carefree, AZ 85377

www.LearningWithLittleFolks.com

Printed by Ave Maria Press, Notre Dame, Indiana

First Printing, 2008

ISBN 978-0-9815500-0-8

Dedicated to the Notre Dame family

Thank you to my fellow members of the
Society of Children's Book Writers and Illustrators in Arizona
for their support
especially Brooke Bessesen for her editorial skills
and BG Hennessy for her artistic direction.

Thank you to John and Sandy McCullough
and to my family — Ed, Kaitlin, Meghan and Michael Greenfield,
for their encouragement in this project.

B.O.G.

Dedicated to the women and men of Notre Dame
who over the many years since I've lived with them on campus
have enriched my life and become my mentors.

I thank Barb for inviting me to be part of this endeavor,
lending artistry to her words
and for the opportunity to become reacquainted with
favorite spots on this beautiful campus.

I also thank those whose images lent a backdrop
for the paintings you'll see on these pages.

J.E.P.

The entire family can enjoy *L is for Leprechaun – an ABC book of Notre Dame*. The simple rhymes accompanied by colorful illustrations appeal to the younger listener while the older child can read fascinating facts and stories in the text. Each letter represents a significant person, place, or event at Notre Dame.

Families can use the book as a tour guide for exploring the University. Pick up a map at the Eck Visitors' Center across from the Bookstore and visit the Campus Stop described for each letter.

If you can't visit Notre Dame, you can experience the sights and sounds at the University's website, www.nd.edu. Take a virtual tour of the campus; visit the Basilica, the Hesburgh Library, or the Jordan Hall of Science. Listen to audio clips of the band playing "The Victory March" and "The Alma Mater." Check out the live webcams of the Dome and the quads.

Go Irish!

The University arboretum was designed in the 1880s under the guidance of Father Sorin. The plan was to plant every tree native to the United States that would grow in the northern Indiana climate. Today the campus is home to fifteen of the fifty largest trees native to St. Joseph County.

When visitors, students, and alumni walk the campus, they realize that Notre Dame is a special place with a colorful history. If buildings could talk, visitors would hear many stories. The Log Chapel would share the prayers of the French missionaries whose dream was to build a Catholic university in the Indiana wilderness. The stadium would echo the cheers for the Fighting Irish football teams. The Hesburgh Library would whisper the hushed words of students cramming for finals. The Jordan Hall of Science would buzz with the excitement of researchers discovering cures for diseases. But, buildings can't talk and yet, these stories need to be told.

Alumnae Barbara Ondercin Gowan and Jane Pitz want children to hear the stories of Notre Dame. Reunited at Reunion 2007, Barbara discovered that her freshman year rector, Jane, was a talented artist and could illustrate her writing. Their collaboration of words and photography resulted in this book that shares the spirit and stories of Notre Dame for all to enjoy.

 **is for Alumni,**
students who earn a degree
by studying hard and graduating
from the University.

Students become members of the Notre Dame family when they enter the University and after graduation the Alumni Association continues to nurture that family spirit. Reunion Weekend is traditionally held the first weekend in June and the campus becomes home again for graduates. Over 260 clubs worldwide offer alumni the opportunity to come together to perform community service projects, attend continuing education seminars, or to cheer on the Fighting Irish at a football watch party. Subway alumni, devoted fans who did not attend the University, often join in the activities. On football weekends, the Eck Visitors' Center and Alumni Association headquarters is a busy spot.

WELCOME
ECK
VISITORS CENTER
AND
Alumni Association
ND
NOTRE DAME

Campus Stop:

Stop by the Eck Visitors' Center to join a student-led campus walking tour or to view a short movie about the University.

B

B is for the **Basilica**,
a house of God and work of art.
The church with the tall spire
is dedicated to the Sacred Heart.

The Basilica of the Sacred Heart is the center for prayer and worship. Father Edward Sorin, the founder and first president of the University, laid the cornerstone for the church in 1871. The priceless stained glass windows, elaborate golden altar, and church bells were imported from France. One of the bells is more than seven feet tall and weighs over six tons. A South Bend carpenter added the spire as payment for his son's education. Vatican artist Luigi Gregori spent four years painting the colorful murals on the walls and vaulted ceiling. The ornate Lady Chapel was added to help celebrate the 50th anniversary of Father Sorin's ordination. Pope John Paul II designated the church as a basilica in 1992.

Campus Stop:
Explore the museum in the basilica sacristy to learn more about the history of Notre Dame.

C is for Champions,
the top rated athletes of the sport,
competing in a boxing ring,
on a football field, or basketball court.

Students grab their bats, balls, clubs, skates, racquets, paddles, swords, and Frisbees and head off to the playing fields and athletic centers around campus to compete in a variety of sports from aikido martial arts to water polo. Each spring over 500 teams of students, faculty, and staff participate in Bookstore Basketball. Varsity athletes have earned national championships in golf, tennis, cross-country, football, fencing, men and women's basketball, and women's soccer. The Fighting Irish football team has earned eleven national championships. It is tradition for every player to touch the sign that reads "Play Like a Champion Today" as they leave the football locker room to take the field at Notre Dame Stadium. The stadium is often referred to as the cradle of champions.

Campus Stop:

Visit the Sports Heritage Hall in the Joyce Center concourse to view old uniforms, equipment, photos, and the National Championship trophies.

D

is for the Dome
shining and glistening gold.
A statue of Mary sits on top.
It's a vision to behold.

The Golden Dome of the Main Building is considered to be the world's most recognized college landmark. It can be seen from miles away. When the Great Fire of 1879 destroyed the Main Building, University founder Father Sorin vowed to rebuild. One hundred days and 4.35 million bricks later, a new building was finished. It was the center of student activity housing dormitories, classrooms, dining halls, and the bookstore. Father Sorin's goal to display a statue of Mary, the mother of God, high atop the dome was realized in 1882. The college women of nearby St. Mary's donated the 19-foot, 4,400-pound statue. Administrators tried to convince Father Sorin to paint the dome yellow but he was stubborn and refused. Finally in 1886, paper-thin strips of gold leaf were carefully applied to the statue and dome. The dome is such a revered symbol that the football team wears gold helmets, the yearbook is named The *Dome*, and graduates refer to themselves as Domers.

Campus Stop:

Tour inside the Main Building to view the colorful murals on the interior of the dome.

E is for Education,
new skills and knowledge
taught by teachers and professors
from grade school through college.

Did you know that many of the first students at Notre Dame were young boys, six to thirteen years old, called minims? In the early days, Notre Dame served as a grade school, high school, trade school, and liberal arts college. Currently over 11,000 students from every state and from over one hundred foreign nations are enrolled in the University undergraduate, graduate, and professional studies programs. International programs are offered in over twenty countries and over 50% of the students study abroad during their college experience. Elderhostel programs led by University professors are offered to senior citizens during the summer.

Campus Stop:

Visit St. Edward's Hall next to the Main Building. It was originally built as the boarding school for the minims.

F
is for **Football**
and the **Four** Horsemen, too.
Legendary players and coaches
dressed in gold and blue.

Imagine 120 boys running up and down the field for two hours. That was Notre Dame football in 1881. Six years later on November 23, 1887, the first varsity game was played against the University of Michigan and that rivalry continues today.

Notre Dame football is made up of legends. In 1913, quarterback Gus Dorais and end Knute Rockne transformed football with the forward pass. During the Golden Age of Notre Dame football, coach Rockne and the team posted a record 105 wins, twelve losses and five ties including five undefeated seasons. Sportswriter Grantland Rice immortalized the backfield of Harry Stuhldreher, Jim Crowley, Don Miller and Elmer Layden when he nicknamed them the Four Horsemen. Under coaches Ara Parseghian, Dan Devine, and Lou Holtz, the Irish won four more national championships.

Campus Stop:

Wander the Rockne Memorial building at the end of the South Quad. It was constructed in 1938.

Grotto begins with the letter **G**.
By the lake, it's a peaceful place.
Light a candle, pray the rosary,
"Hail Mary, full of grace."

The Grotto of Our Lady of Lourdes was built in 1896 using boulders dug out of nearby farm fields. It is a copy of the French cave where the Virgin Mary appeared to the peasant girl Bernadette. Students, faculty, alumni, and visitors often stop at the Grotto to light a candle and kneel in prayer. Before the Michigan football game in 1985, students and visitors lighted over 1,500 candles causing a fire that ignited the shrine and scorched the rocks. The rosary, a special prayer to Mary, is recited daily. The graduating class gathers in prayer during their traditional last visit to the Grotto. The largest tree on campus, a sycamore, shades the Grotto lawn.

Campus Stop:

Light a candle at the Grotto for a special friend.

H
is for Theodore M. Hesburgh, C.S.C. a scholar, leader, and priest, president emeritus, and activist for civil rights and world peace.

Did you know that Father Hesburgh is listed in the *Guinness Book of World Records*? He holds the record for receiving the most honorary college degrees. Theodore Hesburgh left home at the age of seventeen to enter the Holy Cross Seminary at Notre Dame. Nine years later after studying in Rome, he was ordained a priest in Sacred Heart Church. Father Hesburgh served as the University's 15th president from 1952 through 1987. His leadership is evident in government, too. He was honored with the Congressional Gold Medal for his accomplishments in religion, higher education, and civil rights. Father Ted's love of aviation and his adventurous spirit were shown when he flew in the world's fastest jet reaching speeds over 2,200 miles per hour. To celebrate Father Ted's 90th birthday in 2007, students and alumni worldwide performed community service projects in his honor.

Campus Stop: Visit the statue of Fr. Ted and his friend, Fr. Ned Joyce, near the library reflection pool.

I is for the Irish Guard
wearing plaid kilts and standing tall.
They lead the Marching Band
on football weekends in the fall.

The Irish Guard was originally founded as the Irish Pipers in 1949. It was the bagpiper unit in the Marching Band. Since bagpipes do not perform well in cold weather, the instruments were abandoned but the Guard remained as a dignified, precision marching unit. The ten members are required to be a minimum height of six feet two inches but appear much taller in their traditional uniform of red jacket, Notre Dame plaid kilt, and black bearskin shako or hat. High stepping through campus, the Irish Guard leads the band to the stadium and onto the football field. After a Notre Dame win, the Guard dances its famous victory clog to the lively tune "Damsha Bua."

Campus Stop:
On football game day, watch the Irish Guard protect and lead the band from Bond Hall on its march to the stadium.

J is for the JACC,
a sports center of the school.
There is an ice arena, basketball court,
and Olympic-size swimming pool.

The huge twin domes of the Joyce Athletic and Convocation Center or JACC are a campus attraction. It is named for Father Edmund Joyce, University executive vice-president during the Hesburgh years. The JACC or Joyce Center is a hub of athletic activity housing the ice rink, volleyball and basketball courts, and the Rolfs Aquatic Center. The JACC has been the scene of spectacular basketball upsets and winning streaks including several perfect record seasons. The arena explodes with cheers during football pep rallies and has seen famous entertainers such as Elvis Presley, Bob Hope, and U2 perform on its stage.

Campus stop:

Explore the JACC and you may find student athletes practicing on the courts, the rink, or in the pool.

K is for Edward "Moose" Krause

K is for Edward "Moose" Krause known as Mr. Notre Dame, athletic director, coach, and member of the Basketball Hall of Fame.

In 1930 Moose enrolled in Notre Dame after Coach Rockne offered him a football scholarship. He was an All-American tackle on both offense and defense but it was on the basketball court that this talented athlete at six feet three inches was a real giant. Moose was one of the first college athletes to average double figures in points per game and his offensive dominance led to the establishment of the three second rule. Krause returned to Notre Dame in 1942 as assistant coach in both basketball and football. He led the Irish basketball team for six seasons as head coach until 1949 when he took over as the University's athletic director. During his thirty-year tenure as A.D., he saw ten sports reach varsity status including the establishment of women's sports. His service to the University earned him the nickname Mr. Notre Dame.

Campus stop:

Look for the statue of Moose Krause sitting on a bench in front of the Joyce Center.

L is for Leprechaun,
a wee magical man,
Notre Dame's mascot,
and number one fan.

Dressed in a green jacket, knickers, and a country hat, the Leprechaun represents the spirit of the Fighting Irish. At sporting events, this green elf leads cheers, dances the jig, and runs with the ND flag across the field bringing good luck to the team. Since 1964 the Leprechaun has been the official mascot or symbol of the University. The Leprechaun has not always been the mascot. For over thirty years, Irish terriers named Clashmore Mike were the football team's mascot. Today the Leprechaun logo decorates everything from key chains and t-shirts to campus vehicles.

Campus Stop:

Check out the variety of Leprechaun merchandise at the
Hammes Bookstore and Joyce Center Varsity Shops.

M

Marching Band begins with the letter **M**. It's the oldest college band in the nation. Hear them play at football games, parades, and graduations.

UNIVERSITY OF NOTRE DAME MARCHING BAND

Father Sorin loved music and in 1845 purchased a set of instruments. A year later, a student band performed at the first graduation ceremony and The Band of the Fighting Irish has been making music ever since. The band played at the first varsity football game in 1887 and has not missed a single home game since. On game days, the band wakes up the student body as it marches around campus and entertains with a concert on the steps outside Bond Hall before high stepping to the stadium. Football fans sing along to the "Victory March" and are delighted when the band members form the letters for Irish on the field.

Campus Stop:

View memorabilia and displays at the Ricci Band Rehearsal Hall.

Father Charles O'Donnell, Notre Dame president and poet, wrote the lyrics while band director Joseph Casasanta composed the melody of the alma mater. It was first performed at the funeral of football coach Knute Rockne in 1931. In days past, the sound of the carillon bells from Sacred Heart Church playing the alma mater would signal lights out in the dorms. Students today are taught the words during Frosh Orientation. The alma mater is played at weddings and graduations, in churches, and in stadiums. The alma mater is sung at the end of every football game by fans swaying with linked arms. The sentimental words often bring tears to the eyes of alumni – "and our hearts forever, love thee, Notre Dame."

Campus stop:

Listen for the church bells
at 10pm playing
"Notre Dame, our Mother."

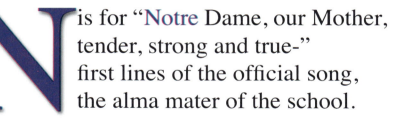

N is for "Notre Dame, our Mother, tender, strong and true-" first lines of the official song, the alma mater of the school.

O is for The *OBSERVER*.
Read the daily news,
business, sports, campus life,
Viewpoint, and movie reviews.

Interested in what's happening on campus this week? Pick up a copy of the daily student newspaper. The *Observer* has served the Notre Dame and St. Mary's community since 1966. The 150 students on staff write, edit, and publish the independent paper. Photographs and even the comic strips are student creations. The *Observer* has been recognized as the College Newspaper of the Year.

There are other student publications. The *Scholastic* is the oldest, continuously published, student magazine in the United States. The *Juggler* magazine focuses on literature and art. The *Dome* yearbook is a photo recap of the year's activities. Students also run local radio and TV stations.

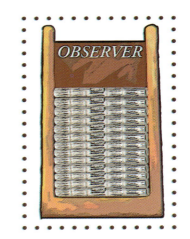

Campus Stop:

Pick up a copy of The *Observer*
at the dining halls,
Bookstore, LaFortune,
or the Morris Inn.

P is for Peace Studies,

classes where students explore how people can live in harmony and put an end to violence and war.

Students from every continent and over ninety countries have earned degrees in the Peace Studies program. The Kroc Institute for International Peace Studies is the world's leading research, teaching, and policy center. Lectures are held on campus and around the world. Many international students return to their homeland with hopes of building peace in their war torn countries.

In addition to the Peace Studies program, students volunteer through the Center for Social Concerns. Over 80% of Notre Dame students are active in service projects such as tutoring children, caring for the elderly, and building homes in Appalachia.

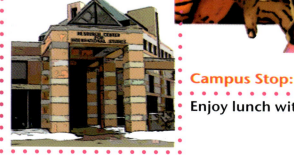

Campus Stop:

Enjoy lunch with an international flavor at the Greenfields Café in the Hesburgh Center for International Studies.

Q is for Quads,
the campus design.
Walkways lead to old buildings
covered in vine.

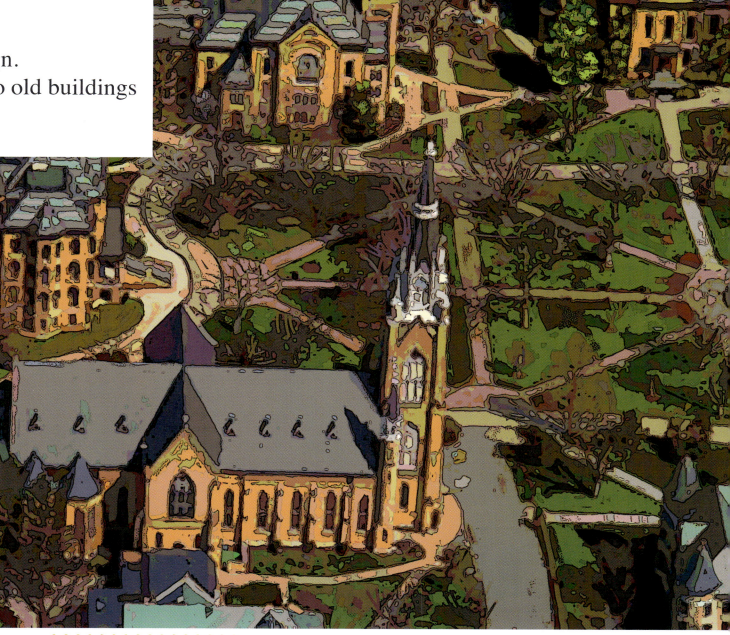

An aerial view reveals that the campus is laid out in quadrangles or large, rectangular, open spaces walled in by buildings on four sides. Father Sorin designed the traditional Main Quad with tree-lined Notre Dame Avenue leading to the Main Building and its Golden Dome. Today students refer to this quad with the Basilica and first University buildings as the God Quad. Towers, turrets, gables, and gargoyles adorn the dorms on the expansive South Quad. North Quad is home to the Clarke Memorial Fountain, a peace memorial nicknamed Stonehenge. The Hesburgh Library towers over the Mod Quad while the Hammes Bookstore sits on the West Quad. The newest quad is busy with students attending lectures in classroom buildings and theater productions in the DPAC, the DeBartolo Center for the Performing Arts.

Campus Stop:

Stop in the Snite Museum of Art on the South Quad.

R is for Research,
to study, experiment, and analyze.
Discover how genes control development
and win the Nobel Prize.

Did you know that a Notre Dame paleontologist unearthed a sixty-six million years old Tyrannosaurus rex fossil or that a theology scholar translated the ancient Dead Sea Scrolls? Biologists search out cures for tropical diseases by studying mosquitoes while anthropologists analyze the sleep patterns of babies and their mothers. Alumni Eric Wieschaus was awarded the 1995 Nobel Prize in Medicine for his research into how genes control development in embryos.

Notre Dame has always focused on research. In the late 1800s, Albert Zahm pioneered early flying machines when he launched homemade gliders from the roof of LaFortune. Father Julius Nieuwland is famous for chemistry experiments that led to the development of synthetic rubber. Today Notre Dame is home to ten major research institutes.

Campus Stop:

Explore the Jordan Hall of Science, home to the Museum of Biodiversity, the Digital Visualization Theater, and laboratories.

S is for Father Sorin,
an ambitious and holy man.
To build a great Catholic university
was his life long plan.

The French missionary from the Congregation of Holy Cross, Father Edward Sorin, was just twenty-eight years old when he arrived in the snowy Indiana wilderness with the goal of establishing the greatest Catholic university in the world. L'Universite´ de Notre Dame du Lac, the University of Our Lady of the Lake, began as a small, two-story brick building that housed a dormitory, classroom, and bakery. Old College is the only original landmark on campus. In addition to University duties, Father Sorin cared for the Catholic families in the surrounding territory and even served as postmaster. Father Sorin is buried near the crucifix in the Holy Cross Community Cemetery near St. Mary's Lake.

Campus Stop:

Look for the statue of Father Sorin on the Main Quad. He holds a book and a crucifix in his hands.

T is for Christ the Teacher
with arms raised high.
He watches over students and visitors
as they pass by.

Decorating the Hesburgh Library tower is the Word of Life mosaic. Saints who were great thinkers and scholars surround the central figure of Christ the Teacher. With arms raised, Christ overlooks the football stadium and is often referred to as "Touchdown Jesus." More than 5,700 pieces of stone from sixteen countries were used to create the 132-foot-high mural visible from the stadium and mirrored in the reflecting pool.

The first library was housed in the Main Building. Today the Hesburgh Library and its branches hold more than 3 million books. A clay tablet written in cuneiform from 2300 BC, a 750-year-old schoolbook and even autographed baseballs are part of the Library's Rare Books and Special Collections.

Campus Stop:

To admire old books and artifacts, visit the Rare Book Room on the main floor of the Hesburgh Library.

U is for University,
where college students study and play,
attend lectures, and write papers
until graduation day.

Founder Father Sorin would be proud to see his University today. As he predicted in 1842, "Before long it will develop on a large scale…It will be one of the most powerful means for doing good in this country."

Notre Dame attracts the brightest students to its four colleges – arts and letters, business, engineering, and science – and schools of architecture, law, and graduate studies. The residence halls house 80% of the undergraduates and are host to activities such as dances, community service projects, talent shows, and interhall athletic teams. There are over sixty chapels on campus. Construction of new residence halls, classrooms, research facilities, and athletic and shopping venues will expand the campus scene.

Campus Stop:

**The LaFortune Student Center is a fun place
to grab a snack and check out sports posters and photos from the past.**

V is for "The Victory March,"
the University's famous fight song. "Cheer, cheer for old Notre Dame" fans sing out loud and strong.

Hum it, sing it, or strum it. "The Notre Dame Victory March" is the most recognized and greatest of all college fight songs. Graduates Michael and John Shea began composing the song on a piano in Sorin Hall in 1908 when they returned to campus for a football game. The next year, it was performed as part of the band's Easter morning concert. The brothers were surprised at the success of their work. In later years, they set out to compose a better song called "The Fighting Team." The new song was not well received and the original lyrics and ragtime tune would become a tradition of Notre Dame. Band members estimate that they play "The Victory March" over 4,000 times each year.

Notre Dame Victory March

Rally sons of Notre Dame:
Sing her glory and sound her fame,
Raise her Gold and Blue
And cheer with voices true:
Rah, rah, for Notre Dame
We will fight in ev-ry game,
Strong of heart and true to her name
We will ne'er forget her
And will cheer her ever
Loyal to Notre Dame

Cheer, cheer for old Notre Dame
Wake up the echoes cheering her name,
Send a volley cheer on high,
Shake down the thunder from the sky.
What though the odds be great or small
Old Notre Dame will win over all,
While her loyal sons are marching
Onward to victory

Campus Stop:
Look in the bookstore for CDs of the Marching Band and the Glee Club performing "The Victory March."

W

W is for Women,
first admitted in 1972.
These daughters of du Lac
proudly wear the gold and blue

September 5, 1972 was a historic day at Notre Dame. After 130 years, the all-male school admitted 365 undergraduate women and the era of coeducation began. Walsh and Badin were the first dorms to be home to women. In the early years, there were only a few females in each classroom but today nearly half of the students are women. Women have adapted well to the Notre Dame traditions. There have been female valedictorians, student body presidents, drum majors, and even members of the Irish Guard.

These were not the first women to receive degrees from Notre Dame, however. During the summers in the 1950s and '60s, religious sisters in their long habits filled the classrooms and dorms earning graduate degrees. Today young women from around the world study at Notre Dame.

Campus Stop:

Look for the rock near the entrance to the cave at the Grotto inscribed with words of thanksgiving from the first women's class.

X marks the spot on the map, an Indian mission near South Bend. Father Sorin's long journey from France would finally come to an end.

A young Father Sorin and six Brothers, one only fourteen years old, sailed from France in 1841 to America. The missionaries spent thirty-nine days in the cramped, dark steerage hold with over fifty others because they were too poor to afford a cabin on the ship. Their travels continued from New York to southern Indiana where the bishop offered them land to build an elementary school. For a year, they ministered to the people, worked hard, and learned English.

Father Sorin's dream was to build a college. With $310 in his pocket, he set out on a 250-mile northward trek over icy roads and frozen rivers. Ten days later, the weary travelers arrived at the south bend of the St. Joseph River where the friendly fur trader Alexis Coquillard met them. On November 26, 1842, Father Sorin set his eyes on the snow-covered site that would become the University of Notre Dame.

Campus stop:

Visit the Log Chapel, a replica of the cabin that served Father Sorin and the missionaries when they first arrived in 1842.

Y is for frozen Yogurt,
a tasty treat to eat.
Served in the dining halls,
it's a dessert that's cold and sweet!

Hungry students eat in the North and South Dining Halls where award-winning chefs cook a variety of healthy meals. Over 2,000 sandwiches, including 400 peanut butter and jelly, are prepared for the student in a hurry at lunch. Candlelight dinners are served on football weekends.

LaFortune Student Center is home to the Huddle Food Court. Reckers, named for the first student to enroll at Notre Dame, is always open and located adjacent to the South Dining Hall. On football game day, the campus is transformed into a giant picnic as clubs set up tables outdoors to raise money selling brats, hamburgers, and even steak sandwiches.

Campus Stop:

The dining halls are open to campus visitors and are a fun place for families to eat.

Z

Z is for Zahm,
a dorm east of the Golden Dome.
Ignats the Moose is mascot
and 240 men call it home.

Zahm residents, or Zahmbies, affectionately refer to their dorm as Zahm House. It was constructed in 1937 on the North Quad and named for the brilliant scientist Father John A. Zahm. During World War II, Zahm Hall housed naval officer candidates while they trained at the University. In the days when upperclassmen with the highest grade point averages got first pick of the dorms, Zahm had the least desirable location on the outskirts of campus and so earned the reputation of housing the most social students. Today dorms are randomly assigned to freshmen but the Zahm men continue traditions demonstrating their dorm spirit and community service.

Campus Stop:

Look for a huge red "Z" hanging from one of the hall's third floor windows and illuminating the North Quad at night.

CAMPUS STOPS

A   Eck Visitors' Center

B   Basilica of the Sacred Heart

C   Sports Heritage Hall, Joyce Center

D   Main Building

E   St. Edward's Hall

F   Rockne Memorial

G   Grotto

H   Reflection pool, Hesburgh Library

I   Bond Hall

J   JACC

K   Moose Krause statue

L   Hammes Bookstore

M   Ricci Band Rehearsal Hall

THE AUTHOR AND THE ARTIST

A member of the first class of women at Notre Dame, Barbara Ondercin Gowan graduated with a Bachelor of Science in Biology in 1976. Following a career as a park naturalist in the Cleveland Metroparks, Barbara and her husband moved to Arizona where they raised two daughters, Meghan and Kaitlin, (and two dogs, Sorin and Rockne!) The family is active in the Notre Dame Club of Phoenix. *L is for Leprechaun* is Gowan's third children's book.

Jane Pitz was recruited in 1972 to assist in opening one of the first women's residence halls at Notre Dame. She lived for almost twenty years with students on campus and in England in the Arts and Letters London Program. She now resides in South Bend where she is able to keep in touch with the unfolding growth of the University. Jane earned a Masters in Fine Arts from Notre Dame and continues to develop her love of art as an illustrator.